To the Earth and Back

By Lora Faris

Illustrations by Sian James

For all mothers.

Thank you to Danielle, Ashley, Carolyn and all of the women in the postpartum support group at
Lee Arrendale State Prison whose bravery made this story possible.

A special thank you to our incredible Motherhood Beyond Bars staff and board. And to Aimee Bosley,
Zachary Carroll, Linh-Yen Hoang, Mairi McCaslin, Taylor Norman, Savana Scarlett-Schuur, and
everyone else who volunteered their time and talents to make this book a reality.

The night you were born, the Earth shone especially bright.

Moon Nursery
Room 2

I held you in my arms, and the cold moon warmed,
its rocky sands softening as I sang you to sleep.

*Twinkle, twinkle, little star,
how I wonder what you are.*

With your tiny hand in mine,
I forgot about my moon mission.
I forgot about the long months ahead.

The night you were born, Princess Moon Baby, you became my whole world.

But then, a static-filled crackle. A radio pop and a hiss.

"Ship now arriving for Princess Moon Baby.
Takeoff to Earth scheduled for oh-nine-hundred."

I begged, I pleaded, and I held you tight.

"Astronauts.   Don't.   Cry."

"I'm sorry, Princess Moon Baby."
And with that, the moon went cold, and the Earth lost its shine.

"I love you to

he Earth and back."

With a heavy heart, I climbed into my rover.
With empty arms, I headed back to base.

Collapsing into my spacebunk, I felt more alone than ever.

But there you were, a beacon of light in a desolate place.

"Time for work, Astronaut."

The next dozen moon days dragged like

a   hundred   Earth   years.

I tried to tell myself:
Astronauts.
Don't.
Cry.

But I wasn't just an astronaut. I was your Mama.

I am your Mama.

I type you letters.

Make toys out of space junk.

Collect moon rocks in funny shapes.

Each gift one day closer to being with you.

When I fill my bags with one hundred treasures,
when butterflies fill my stomach and stars fill the sky,

I fly home to you.

The landing gear goes bump, bump, bump...
Or is that my heart?

Princess Moon Baby, do you remember me?

Tonight, the moon shines:
Especially bright.

About the book

To the Earth and Back began as a series of intimate interviews with mothers both formerly and currently incarcerated. From there, it was transformed into an epic story representative of their love, strength, and fortitude. There is no singular story to tell about giving birth while incarcerated, but we set out to make sure that each interviewee's experience was reflected in some way, big or small.

Carolyn's interview gave us one of the largest pieces of inspiration in the form of Angel Princess Baby, the nickname she gave to her daughter in the delivery room. But while the nickname was unique, the circumstances of the delivery were disappointingly common.

Carolyn only had two hours to spend with Angel Princess Baby, and begging for more time resulted in a callous statement from prison staff that several of our mothers have been told over the years:

"Football players don't cry."

But mothers do.

We thank all of these women for trusting us with their stories and for allowing us to be stewards of both their joy and their trauma. And we thank you, dear reader, for showing these mothers that their stories and experiences matter.

To learn more about our mission at Motherhood Beyond Bars and to learn about how you can further support our work, visit MotherhoodBeyond.org

Thank you to all of our Kickstarter donors, especially:

Cassie & John Powell · Stacy Kemp · Bob & Anne Carroll · Marie Martin · June, Molly & Nate · Kennedy, Ava & Andrew Hilson · Mary Fraser Kirsh · Sara J. Totonchi · Madelyn McCaslin · The Edwards family · Elain Ellerbe, Mathe family & Refined By Fire Ministries · Amelia Dunlop · Sarah Price of Neon Cardigan · Arden & Walter Rowland · Isaac Clemens

Motherhood Beyond Bars

CPSIA information can be obtained
at www.ICGtesting.com
Printed in the USA
LVRC101123280422
717082LV00033BA/622